What Happened When Grandma Died

by Peggy Barker

Illustrated by Patricia Mattozzi

The Bible texts in this publication are from the Good News Bible, the Bible in TODAY'S ENGLISH VERSION. Copyright © American Bible Society 1966, 1971, 1976. Used by permission.

3558 S. Jefferson Avenue, St. Louis, MO 63118
Manufactured in China

11 12 13 14 15 03 02

To my daughter
Jennifer Susan
and to my grandchildren
Elisabeth, Esther, Sarah,
Ginny, Katy,
John, and Charity
and
the many other children
who may wonder,
when death takes someone
very near and very dear
just what happens
to their grandma
when God calls her home

Last Monday my grandma died. She was out in her garden pruning her bushes when she died.

When my mom told me about it, I felt so bad. I cried and cried. She hugged me tight and said she felt bad, too.

The next day our family took our van and drove south to Grandma's for the funeral. On the way we talked about my grandma and what it meant to die. This is how my dad explained it:

"When Grandma died she left behind three things," said my dad. "They were things that were very old. They were things she would never need again.

"First, she left behind her body. That was the part of her that made her look the way she did. She had always been very strong and well, but she was 81 years old. I guess her body was tired, and it just wore out.

"Second, she left behind her old home. It was a pretty white house with a big porch in front and a little porch in back. It had lots of neat things in it and flowers all around it. It was a comfortable old house—not too fancy, not too plain. It was just the right place for Grandma. But she won't live there any more."

The other thing dad said Grandma left behind was her old life, and that life hadn't always been easy. Grandma had worked hard all her life. She had never had a lot of money. She never got to travel many places. And lately her hands and knees had become stiff and hurty, the way many old people's hands and knees seem to get.

But Grandma's life was full of good times, too. She enjoyed being with her family, doing things with her friends, and helping at church. She especially enjoyed tending her plants and garden—and making pretty things with her hands.

She was a busy lady and a happy lady. She knew lots of people and she laughed a lot with them. They all seemed to like her—and liked to be with her.

But the best part of Grandma's life was her knowing and loving Jesus. She knew that Jesus loved her because He gave His life for her. She called Him her Savior.

Because Grandma trusted in Jesus as her Savior, she also knew that she would be with God in heaven when she died.

Do you know what God promised Grandma—and promises all believers—about heaven? My dad said that God promises three new things!

God promises three new things.

IN LOVING MEMORY OF
MRS. EDWARD RICHARDSON

God will give Grandma a new body. I don't know exactly what it will be like, but it will be her. And the Bible says it will never hurt or get tired or get sick or grow old or die. Her new body will never wear out.

The Bible says, "God will wipe away all tears from their eyes. There will be no more death, no more grief or crying or pain. The old things have disappeared." *Revelation 21:4*

Dad said that the Bible promises us that God has given Grandma a new home in heaven . . . a new place to live. She is living in it right now. And she will always be happy there.

"There are many rooms in My Father's house, and I am going to prepare a place for you. . . . And after I go and prepare a place for you, I will come back and take you to Myself, so that you will be where I am." *John 14:2-3*

And God has given Grandma one more thing—a new life. In her new life she is happy and busy praising and loving and thanking God. She will be doing things to enjoy God and to make Him happy. Maybe she is even making an afghan with colors from the rainbow!

"You will show me the path that leads to life; Your presence fills me with joy and brings me pleasure forever." *Psalm 16:11*

God has given Grandma this new life, and it will go on for ever and ever, because God's gift of new life never ends.

Soon we went to the funeral place, and there we saw Grandma's "old" body. It looked like she was just sleeping. Many friends were there. Some of them were sad. That was because they would miss their friend and the part of their lives they shared together. Some friends were telling each other the things they like to remember about Grandma. They seemed happy doing that.

Later on we went to her church, and we had a worship service. Someone sang a gentle song. They read from the Bible. The pastor talked and then he prayed. Then we all sang a song of praise to God for the way He loves and cares for us all through our lives.

I know I'll miss my grandma. She was a special friend to me. But I know I'll see her in heaven someday, because *I* love Jesus, too.

And I know I'm glad that God is taking care of her
in her new home
and her new life.

A Message to Parents

As we faced the impending deaths of a grandfather and a next-door neighbor—both believers in Jesus as their Savior, both advanced in their illnesses, and both very near and dear, we wondered how we would present the facts of death in a Christian context to our retarded daughter, who knew and loved both people very much.

Then suddenly and unexpectedly God called home a very dear aunt in another state, Aunt Georgie, as she was out in her garden early one morning, pruning her raspberry bushes.

As I asked God for wisdom to prepare our daughter for the experiences ahead of us, He graciously helped my thoughts to get organized into the perspective this book presents. We had a six-hour drive to the funeral, and during those precious hours we were able to introduce her, step by step, to the three *old things* of Aunt Georgie's life, which we were certain to see, and to show her God gave to Aunt Georgie three *new things* in comparable categories which are infinitely better in heaven.

So comfortably and completely did she take in the explanations we gave her, that upon arriving at the funeral parlor our daughter of her own accord approached the coffin, gazed pensively at her aunt's still form and said, "That's Aunt Georgie's *old* body."

Within a month the two dear people mentioned earlier joined Aunt Georgie in heaven. It was Jennifer who sat down by her grandmother and quietly told her about Grandfather's *three old things* and the *three new things* he would receive from God. Later on she shared the experience in church with her youth group, and she helped one child who was facing his grandmother's death to receive the same comfort she had received from God through us (2 Corinthians 1:3-4).

We praise God for our daughter whose handicap forced us to take a "simple look at profound truths" and to express them in clear terms that can be shared equally well with an adult or child—and by an adult or a child.

Peggy Barker